KEIKO KANAO

Kitten Up a Tree

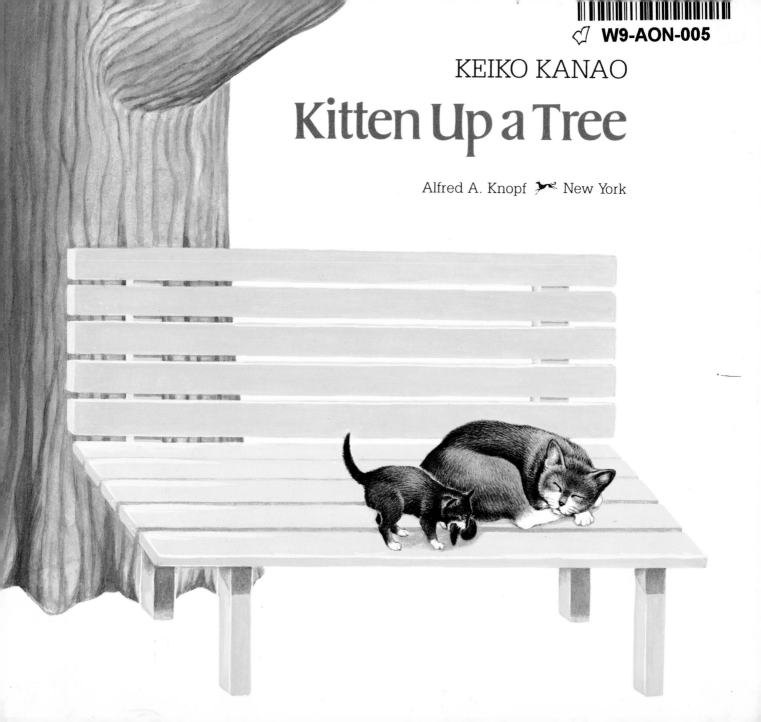

Alfred A. Knopf • New York

What's that flying
so close to the tree?
Kitten wants to find out.

She climbs up after it…

higher and higher…

but it flies away.

Now Kitten is stuck
up in the tree.
    She is afraid to
climb down by herself.

"Mee-yow!" she cries.
"Help me, Mama!"

Kitten's mother wakes up.

She leaps off the bench
and onto the tree.

Then she climbs
right up to Kitten.

"Don't cry, Kitten,"
she says. "There is
nothing to be afraid of."

And she carries
Kitten down.

"My goodness," says Mama. "What an adventure you have had today!"

Kitten is very happy to be safe and sound again.